Magic Pony Carousel
Book 1

SPARKLE
THE CIRCUS PONY

Poppy Shire

Illustrations by Ron Berg

HarperCollins_Publishers_

With thanks to Gill Harvey

HarperTrophy® is a registered trademark of
HarperCollins Publishers.

★ ★ ★ ★ ★

SPARKLE THE CIRCUS PONY

Text copyright © 2007 by Working Partners

Illustrations copyright © 2007 by Ron Berg

www.harpercollinschildrens.com

Library of Congress Cataloging-in-Publication Data
Shire, Poppy.
Sparkle the circus pony / Poppy Shire ; illustrated by Ron
Berg.— 1st ed.
p.   cm.— (The magic pony carousel ; bk. 1)
Summary: Megan goes for a ride on a magic carousel that
takes her to a circus where she and her pony are the star per-
formers in Mr. Scarletti's Amazing Traveling Circus. Includes
facts about circuses.
ISBN-10: 0-06-083779-9
ISBN-13: 978-0-06-083779-2
[1. Circus—Fiction. 2. Ponies—Fiction. 3. Space and
time—Fiction.] I. Berg, Ron, ill. II. Title. III. Series.
PZ7.S55795Sp 2006   2006000369
[Fic]—dc22   CIP
                                                    AC

Typography by Sasha Illingworth

❖

First Harper Trophy edition, 2007

★ ★ ★ ★ ★

Chapter 1

"Step up, step up for the most exciting ride of your lives! Choose your favorite pony and let Barker's Magic Pony Carousel whisk you away on an amazing adventure!"

Megan felt tingly all over when she heard the voice booming across the fairground. A Magic Pony Carousel? She couldn't think of anything more wonderful!

"*That's* the ride I'd like to go on next!" she told her mom. "Can I, please?"

"I thought you didn't like ponies anymore,"

her mom teased. "That's what you said when you fell off in your riding lesson last week."

Megan thought for a moment. It was true that falling off had made her a bit nervous about *real* ponies. "But carousel ponies will be a lot safer," she said.

"Yes, they will," agreed her mom. "Though I'm not sure why you're worried about ponies when you're so crazy about gymnastics. That's just as dangerous, if you ask me!"

Megan laughed. "Oh, no," she said. "In gymnastics there are nice thick mats to land on!"

The Magic Pony Carousel stood in a far corner of the field, next to a cotton candy stand. The base was painted in swirling patterns of red, gold, and silver, and twinkling colored lights hung from the roof. The horses were fixed to twisty golden poles, rising up and down in time with the music. Megan thought she'd never be able to decide which one to ride. They all looked lovely. There was a beautiful chestnut Arab horse with a pretty star and a flowing mane and tail . . . a majestic bay knight's charger dressed for battle . . . a pretty Appaloosa with a Western saddle and bridle. . . .

And then she saw the fourth horse, which had a feathery pink headdress that sparkled in the twinkling lights. He had no saddle or reins at all, and his dappled back looked smooth and comfortable. His neck was proudly arched, but his big brown eyes were warm and friendly and his snow-white tail streamed out behind him.

"It's a circus pony!" Megan breathed. She

could already imagine herself under the bright lights in a circus ring, wearing a spangly sequined costume.

She left her mom and ran over for a closer look. There was a name written on a scroll hanging from the twisty pole.

"'Sparkle,'" Megan read. "Perfect."

As she gazed up at the pony, she felt a tickle in her nose. It grew and grew and grew until Megan couldn't stop it. *"Ahhh-choo!"* she sneezed.

"Bless you!" cried a voice.

Megan spun around. A tall man was smiling down at her. He looked very different from the other fairground people. He was wearing a red velvet suit with a bright green lining and a stripy green-and-red top hat, with wisps of white hair peeping from underneath.

"I am Mr. Barker," he announced with a bow. "And this is my world-famous Magic Pony Carousel. Here, take a hanky." He pulled a whole string of colored handkerchiefs out of his pocket.

"Wow!" gasped Megan. "Thank you!" She picked out a pink hanky with yellow flowers.

"Have you chosen which pony you're going to ride?" asked Mr. Barker, his blue eyes twinkling merrily.

"Oh yes." Megan nodded.

Mr. Barker held up his hand. "Don't tell me!" he warned. "Just close your eyes and think very hard about the pony you want."

"Go on, Megan," her mom encouraged her.

Megan squeezed her eyes tight shut and pictured Sparkle's shiny white coat and gorgeous pink headdress.

"Are you thinking hard?" asked Mr. Barker.

"*Very* hard," Megan replied.

"Then open your eyes and take a ticket. You don't need to pay—my Magic Carousel is free to everyone!"

To Megan's astonishment, an old-fashioned ticket machine had appeared in front of her on a little red stand. She was *sure* it hadn't been there before. She glanced at her mom to see if she'd noticed it, but she was busy rummaging in her bag. Megan turned back to Mr. Barker, who smiled and turned a wooden handle on the side of the machine. A little pink ticket popped out.

"Is that for me?" Megan exclaimed.

"It most certainly is," said Mr. Barker. "Go on, see which pony the Magic Carousel has chosen for you!"

Megan took the ticket and looked down at the swirly silver writing. Then she gave a little cry of joy. The ticket said **Sparkle**.

She was going to ride the circus pony!

Megan climbed eagerly onto Sparkle's back. She felt very daring, riding bareback, but she was sure she wouldn't fall off, because she could hold on to the twisty golden pole. She waved to her mom with one hand as the carousel began to turn.

The carousel ponies rose and fell in time to the tinkling music. It felt wonderful, like flying gently through the air. Megan held on more tightly as the carousel spun faster. She caught one more glimpse of her mom's smiling face, then all she could see were the dazzling colors of the carousel. Was she imagining it, or had they got brighter? She could even see twinkling stars in her pony's headdress!

The fairground vanished in a blur of pink and silver glitter. This was the most amazing ride Megan had ever been on! She tried to grip the pole tighter, then stared in surprise. She wasn't holding the pole. She was holding Sparkle's mane, and there was silky hair between her fingers, as if it was a *real* mane. She let go with one hand and stroked Sparkle's neck. It felt soft and warm. And then she heard something new—just like the rhythm of horses' hooves. . . .

Megan gasped. What had happened to the carousel pony? The pink and silver sparkles began to fade away, and Megan thought she could see another white pony just like Sparkle in front of her. Before she could be sure, she felt herself wobble. She grabbed on to the mane and looked down.

Sparkle's hooves were thudding on pale

yellow sawdust, around a ring enclosed by scarlet-painted wood. Puzzled, Megan looked around. A dark blue canvas roof stretched above them, decorated with tiny silver stars.

She was riding a real pony in a circus ring!

The last of the sparkles vanished, and Megan could see everything clearly. Sparkle was following five other white ponies around the ring, all wearing a twinkling blue head-dress. Megan thought Sparkle was prettier than all the others. He was the only one with a pink headdress, too. The other riders were wearing brightly colored leotards and leggings, with soft dance shoes on their feet. Megan looked down, and her eyes almost popped out of her head. She was wearing the same things!

Before she could wonder where her jeans

and jacket had gone, she realized that the other riders weren't sitting on their ponies anymore. One by one, they tucked up their feet and crouched on their ponies' backs. After their ponies cantered a few strides, they got their balances and stood up with their arms held out to the sides.

Megan gulped. Was she supposed to copy them? She'd done hardly any riding before. But she was cantering around the ring on a circus pony, so she guessed she had to try! At least she was good at balancing from all her gymnastics, and luckily no one was watching. The seats in the circus ring were empty, and the other riders weren't looking back.

Slowly, carefully, she lifted her feet up one at a time until she was crouching, as she'd seen the other riders do. So far, so good! Then she let go of Sparkle's mane, and began to straighten her legs, so that she was rising up, up, up. . . .

She wobbled first one way, then the other.

"Oh!" Megan gasped, stretching out her arms.

That made it a bit easier to balance. Feeling safer, she straightened her legs the rest of the way. She was standing on the back of a real live circus pony!

But then she glanced down at Sparkle's ears. They didn't seem quite straight. Not at all straight. In a single split second, Megan realized she'd lost her balance after all. She was falling, falling. . . .

Thump.

She was off!

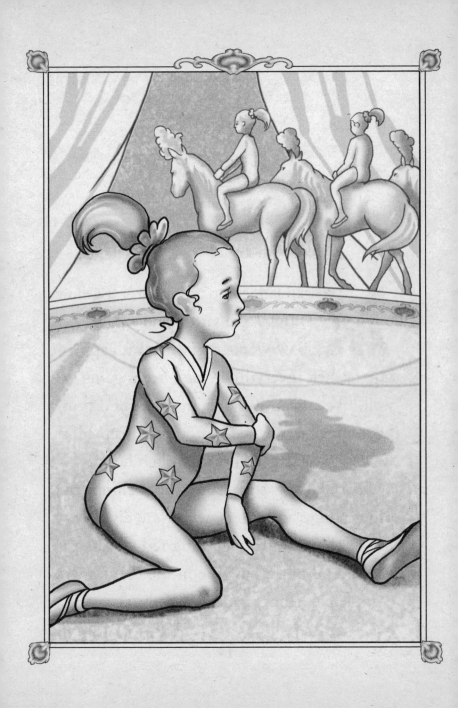

Chapter 2

Megan landed on a heap of soft yellow sawdust. She sat up and rubbed her elbow, wondering what was happening to her. Everything had been going so well, like a beautiful dream, then she'd tumbled off! She frowned. *Was* this a dream? If it was, why hadn't the bump woken her up?

Sparkle was still cantering behind the other ponies and riders, who were disappearing one by one through long red curtains at the far end of the ring. Soon the big top was completely empty, and the velvet curtains swished shut. Tiers of seats stretched away into the shadows near the star-spotted roof. This wasn't part of the fairground, was it? Wherever Megan was, she had to get back to the carousel before her mom realized she'd disappeared!

Megan wondered if she should follow the ponies through the curtains—but then Sparkle trotted over. He was the only pony left in the ring.

He stopped in front of Megan and pricked his ears. "Are you all right down there?" he said in a young, friendly voice.

Megan's mouth fell open. "You—you can talk!" she stammered.

Sparkle snorted. "Of course I can."

"But you're a carousel pony!" Megan said. "At least you were a few minutes ago."

"Yes, but it's a *magic* carousel," Sparkle

explained, his big brown eyes shining. "Remember Mr. Barker's ticket machine? And the ticket with my name on it? That didn't just happen by luck. The magic chose you specially. There's something very important for you to do here before you can go back."

Megan tried to take it in. "But what about my mom? She doesn't know where I am!"

"You don't need to worry about that," said Sparkle. "She won't even notice you've gone. You're in magic time here. When you go back to the fairground, your mom will think you've been on the carousel the whole time."

"Wow!" Megan's mouth dropped open. She scrambled to her feet. "But how am I going to get home?" she asked.

"The magic will take you back when the special task is over," Sparkle reassured her.

"We'll go back together."

Megan looked into Sparkle's eyes with their long black eyelashes, and felt sure she could trust him. "So where am I? What do I have to do?"

"This is Mr. Scarletti's Amazing Traveling Circus," Sparkle replied. "To be honest, I'm not sure what the task is yet. We'll have to find that out together."

It was all very mysterious, and Megan felt a thrill of excitement.

Sparkle nuzzled her arm. "Shall we look around?"

Megan reached out and stroked Sparkle's nose. His muzzle was soft and warm, and felt lovely. "Do you *promise* that my mom won't notice I'm not on the carousel anymore?" she said.

"Promise." Sparkle nodded, making his

headdress twinkle in the big-top lights.

"So what will happen if we run across the ring and out through the curtain?" Megan asked.

"Let's find out!" said Sparkle.

Megan ran across the sawdust and pulled back the red curtain. It was a bright sunny day outside. And spread out all around her was a bustling, colorful circus showground!

Chapter 3

"My, oh my, who's this?" cried a voice. Megan spun around. Standing in front of her was a tall man in a smart scarlet coat—and he looked just like Mr. Barker! He had exactly the same twinkling blue eyes and white hair.

"H-hello," she stammered.

"Welcome to my circus!" said the man, giving her a big, warm smile.

"Are you Mr. Scarletti?" Megan asked, feeling baffled.

"That's right," said the man. "Have a

wonderful time here. I'm sure you will."

He winked and strode away. Megan stared after him. *Was* that Mr. Barker? Surely it couldn't be. How could Mr. Scarletti and Mr. Barker be the same person? It didn't make sense!

She heard a whinny, and realized that Sparkle was waiting for her. Megan turned to follow him and nearly ran straight into a pair of bright red trousers covered in big gold stars.

"Out of my way! Out of my way!" someone shouted.

Just in time, Megan jumped sideways.

"You need to stop daydreaming," called a grumpy voice from high in the air.

Megan looked up. It was the longest pair of trousers she'd ever seen! A man with curly black hair was frowning down at her. Before she had time to apologize, he stalked past, taking giant steps.

"Don't worry about him," said a man in a leopard-skin leotard. "That's Sticky the Stilt-walker. He's *always* grumpy. Even on a good day."

Sparkle nudged her with his muzzle. "Come on, let's see what else there is," he said.

Megan frowned. The gymnast had said, "Even on a good day." Did that mean today was a *bad* day? But before she could ask, Sparkle had trotted off toward a group of six jugglers, and Megan had to run to catch up.

The jugglers were taking stripy wooden clubs out of a colorful trunk labelled THE JOLLY JUGGLERS. They stood in a circle and started throwing the clubs to each other. But even though they caught every one perfectly, they looked miserable. Their shoulders drooped and their mouths turned down at the corners.

"You'd think they'd look a bit happier with a name like that!" said Megan.

Sparkle snorted in agreement, then trotted past and stopped by a rather tangled-looking heap on a mat.

Megan stared. What was *that*? The heap began to move, and all of a sudden it had two legs, two arms, and a head. It wasn't a heap at all but a pretty girl with dark brown skin and little black braids.

The girl looked up at Megan. "Hello," she said in a doleful voice. "Who are you? I haven't seen you around before."

Megan was taken by surprise. She hadn't expected anyone to ask her questions. What if someone asked her where she'd come from?

"Er—I'm Megan," she said. She smiled nervously. "Who are you?"

"Carrie the Contortionist," said the girl. She smiled sadly. "I'm always tied up in knots." Then she looked at Sparkle. "Whisper, what are you doing here? You should be with the other ponies!"

Sparkle lowered his head and snorted. "She thinks I'm one of the circus ponies," he said to Megan. "Come on, we'd better go."

Megan waved good-bye to Carrie and followed Sparkle, her mind buzzing. "Didn't Carrie hear what you just said?" she asked the pony, once they'd left the contortionist behind.

Sparkle shook his mane. "No one here understands me when I speak—apart from you," he said. "They just hear snorts and whinnies. It's all part of the magic."

Megan laughed in delight. She could hardly believe it—a wonderful magical pony all to herself! But in spite of her excitement, she couldn't help noticing how miserable everyone else seemed to be. She followed Sparkle past a group of gloomy trapeze artists, some doleful dancers doing the splits, and a puppeteer with a sad, floppy puppet. Megan frowned. It *must* be a bad day. So far, she hadn't seen a single person who looked happy!

Suddenly, something bounced in front of her and she stopped in surprise. It was an acrobat dressed in a bright pink leotard doing three backflips, all in a row. Megan and Sparkle had come to an open space filled with big rubber mats. Another acrobat was standing on his head, while a third ran around on her hands. Megan wished she could join in!

Eight more acrobats walked onto the mats. Megan waited excitedly to see what they were going to do. First three strong-looking men stood in a row and linked arms. Then a girl with glossy blond hair tied in a ponytail climbed up and balanced on their shoulders.

"It's a human pyramid!" Megan gasped.

Next, a boy about Megan's age stepped forward. He had a mischievous face and his ears stuck out from underneath his untidy black hair. He took a deep breath and heaved himself up to stand next to the girl. He managed to get his feet into position, then stopped. He bent over so that he could cling onto the acrobats underneath.

"That's it, Joshua! Take Sally's hand," called a voice. Megan noticed another girl watching from beside the mats. She looked

about Megan's age, with the same black hair as Joshua, only tidier. She had one arm in a sling.

Joshua looked very nervous. He let go with one hand. Then he let go with the other. But as soon as he began to stand up, everything went wrong.

First he wobbled. Then he gave a yell. Then he lost his balance altogether and toppled over backward, landing with a thump on the rubber mats.

Megan almost giggled. The boy looked so funny with his feet in the air—and when he stood up, his hair was sticking out in tufts all over the place. But she didn't laugh, because everyone else looked so upset.

"Never mind," called out the girl with black hair. "You can do it, Josh! Really, you can!"

"I don't think I can." Joshua sighed.

Sparkle gave Megan a nudge. "Maybe we should say hello to the girl with the sling," he whispered. "We're here to help someone, remember."

With a flick of his tail, he led Megan around the mats to the girl with the injured arm. She looked surprised when she saw Sparkle. "Hello, Whisper. What are you doing here?" she said.

Sparkle looked innocent and turned to Megan. "Come on, Megan, say something," he said, nuzzling the girl's good arm. "You've got to help me out!"

Megan took a deep breath and stepped forward. "Hello," she said. "I'm Megan. I'm sorry you've hurt your arm."

The girl looked puzzled. "Hi," she said. "I'm Juliet. Have you just joined the circus?"

"Not exactly," Megan said. "I'm . . . visiting. Is Joshua your brother? You look just like him."

Juliet smiled. "Actually, he's my twin," she said. Her smile faded. "Poor Josh. He's been trying to learn this routine for ages, so that the acrobats can use it in our gala performance. But it isn't going very well."

Joshua was getting ready to try again, and Megan watched him anxiously. Would he manage to stand up properly this time? One foot was in place. Then the other. Joshua rested his hands on the acrobats' heads for balance. Then slowly, carefully, he straightened his knees.

"Go on! You can do it!" called Juliet.

For a moment, it looked as though maybe he could. A big grin spread across his face as he realized he was actually standing up.

"I've done . . . !" he began.

But he spoke too soon. First he swayed forward, then back. He waved his arms in giant circles, but it didn't help. He fell and landed in a crumpled heap on the mats. This time Megan didn't feel like laughing at all. Everyone looked disappointed as Joshua got to his feet, hanging his head.

"Oh dear," said Megan. Joshua didn't seem to be a very natural acrobat. "Did you hurt your arm in the tumbling act?" she asked Juliet. Maybe both twins had been having trouble with the routine.

Juliet looked so upset that Megan thought she was about to cry. "No," she said. "I'm a rider. I've sprained my wrist." Her bottom lip trembled. "My pony Moonlight stumbled and went lame while we were practicing, and I fell off. It's almost the end of the season and it's our final gala performance tomorrow night. Moonlight and I are supposed to be the stars of the show!"

Megan felt very sorry for Juliet. "Isn't there anyone who can take your place?" she asked.

Juliet shook her head. "There are no other girls to do my routine," she said. "And anyway, Moonlight's still lame. None of the other ponies know our tricks, either."

No wonder everyone was looking so unhappy! The only person Megan had seen looking cheerful was Mr. Scarletti. He hadn't seemed worried at all when he welcomed Megan to his circus. In fact, he had been *very* welcoming. She looked at Sparkle. He wasn't looking upset, either. His ears were pricked and his brown eyes twinkled.

Megan hesitated. Surely this couldn't be

the task she was supposed to do? But then Sparkle gave an encouraging whinny, and she found herself speaking up.

"Oh!" she gasped, looking excitedly at Juliet. "Maybe *I* could take your place!"

Chapter 4

As soon as the words were out, Megan clapped her hand over her mouth. How could she take Juliet's place? She was still a bit scared of riding, and anyway, she kept falling off.

But Juliet was looking curious. "*Could* you?" she asked. "Have you done circus tricks before?"

Megan went bright red. Of course she hadn't done any circus tricks. She didn't know what to say.

But Sparkle seemed excited. He whinnied

and shook his mane. "Tell her you're good at learning," he suggested. "I'll help you with the riding. You'll be perfect, Megan. I'm sure this is why we've come!"

Megan thought for a moment. She loved performing, and the chance to wear a sparkling circus costume instead of a dark blue leotard was too good to be true! "Well," she said. "I *do* ride—a bit. And I've had to learn lots of different gymnastics tricks for displays at school, so I'm sure I could learn circus tricks as well."

Juliet's eyes lit up. "Really?" she exclaimed. Then her face fell. "But who will you ride?"

Megan put her arm around Sparkle's neck. "Sparkle. He's my own pony and he's very clever. I know he looks like one of your circus ponies, but he isn't."

Juliet looked at Sparkle in wonder, then

back at Megan and back at Sparkle again.

"Only you mustn't tell anyone," Megan carried on, lowering her voice. "You have to let everyone else think he's Whisper."

Juliet nodded eagerly. She seemed thrilled to be in on a secret. "Of course," she said. "I won't give him away. I just hope you can both learn my tricks in time."

Sparkle tossed his head. "Hurray!" he said. "This is going to be fun!"

The acrobats finished their practice session, and Joshua walked over to Juliet and Megan, looking completely fed up. Even his tufty hair drooped.

"Don't be sad, Joshua," said Megan. "We've got some good news!"

"Don't tell me. The whole show's been canceled?" Joshua said gloomily.

Juliet ruffled Joshua's hair with her good

hand, making it stick up again. "No. It's *really* good news," she said, laughing. "Meet Megan. She might be able to take my place in the grand finale!"

Joshua's mouth dropped open. "Hey!" he exclaimed. "That's not just good news. It's *great* news!"

Suddenly Megan felt very nervous. What if she fell off in the ring? Then she felt Sparkle blowing gently on her hair.

"Don't worry!" he whispered. "It's all going to be fine!"

Juliet and Joshua were counting on her. Megan knew she couldn't back down. She'd just have to be very, very brave and work hard to learn the tricks.

"Well, I'll try my best," she said. She put her hand on Sparkle's soft warm neck. "We both will."

Sparkle rested his muzzle on her shoulder, and even though he didn't say anything, Megan knew he agreed.

Juliet took Megan's hand. "Let's go to the big top," she said. "It's empty at the moment. You can start practicing."

"Good luck!" called Joshua. "I'll come over later to see how you're doing."

Megan followed Juliet and Sparkle across the showground. Her tummy was fizzing with excitement and nerves. They walked through the red curtain and stopped in the middle of the ring.

"Maybe I could watch you ride for a few minutes," said Juliet. "Then I'll explain how I do my tricks."

Megan nodded. Then she frowned. Sparkle didn't have a saddle and stirrups to help Megan climb onto his back, like the ponies in her riding school. There wasn't a mount-ing block, either. "How am I going to get on?" she asked.

Juliet looked puzzled. "I just vault on," she said. "Don't you do that?"

"I do vaulting in gymnastics," Megan said. "But I've never vaulted onto a pony."

The circus pony arched his neck and snorted, then reached his nose out toward Megan. "Come on!" he urged her. "Try it!"

"I think he wants you to try." Juliet laughed. "Anyone would think he knows exactly what we're talking about!"

Megan grinned. She couldn't tell Juliet that Sparkle was joining in the conversation. She looked into the pony's soft brown eyes and stroked his nose. She knew she could trust him to take care of her. She walked around to his side and placed her hands at the end of his neck on his withers. His back seemed a long way up. Megan bent her knees and jumped, but her feet didn't get any higher than Sparkle's tummy. How could she ride in the gala performance if she couldn't even get on?

"Kick up your right leg so you can swing it over Sparkle's back," said Juliet.

Megan took a deep breath and got ready to try again. Suddenly, she realized Sparkle's back was getting lower.

"He's kneeling down!" Juliet exclaimed.

Sparkle settled down on the sawdust with his legs tucked under him. "Oh, Sparkle," Megan gasped. "You're *wonderful*!"

"He must have guessed you couldn't vault up," said Juliet. "You said he was clever, but I didn't think he would be *that* clever."

Megan wished she could tell Juliet the

truth—that Sparkle was even more clever than she realized. Instead, she held on to his silky mane and climbed onto his back, which was easy now that he was kneeling down. Once she was settled comfortably, Sparkle carefully stood up again. Megan patted his neck.

"I think that counts as your first trick!" Juliet said with a grin.

Sparkle cantered steadily around the ring. Megan decided to try standing up again. Very slowly, she pulled her feet up onto Sparkle's back and crouched there, holding on to his mane.

"Remember to lean into the circle," said Sparkle, puffing a bit because he was cantering. "It will help you to balance."

Megan was too nervous to reply.

One finger at a time, she let go of his mane and straightened her legs. She'd done it!

Then she felt herself wobble. Her feet were slipping on Sparkle's glossy back.

"I'm going to fall!" she cried.

Just as she began to tip sideways, Sparkle swerved the same way, and Megan found herself standing upright again. "Thanks, Sparkle," she whispered.

"Bravo!" cried Juliet, clapping her hands.

After a few more circuits, Megan felt much more confident. "I think I'm ready to try some of your tricks, Juliet," she called. She carefully sat back down on Sparkle's back and rode over to the edge of the ring.

"We'll start with the umbrella trick," Juliet said. She ran behind the red curtain and came back with a beautiful silver umbrella decorated with pink glitter. "You have to open it up and twirl it by the handle so the patterns spin. Then pass it from hand to hand and around your back."

Megan nodded. That sounded easy! She reached down and took the umbrella from Juliet, and Sparkle began cantering around the ring again. Once he was moving in a nice, steady rhythm, Megan stood up on his back, holding the umbrella in one hand.

"Try twirling it first," Juliet called.

Megan looked down at the umbrella. That made her wobble, and she quickly looked straight ahead again. Maybe she could spin the umbrella without looking at it. But when she tried, she wobbled again. It was much harder to balance when she couldn't hold her arms out sideways.

"Try holding the umbrella closer to your body," Juliet suggested.

"I don't think I can," said Megan, beginning to panic. "Sparkle, stop!" Megan sat back down on Sparkle's back. With a snort, Sparkle slowed down and stopped at the edge of the ring.

Juliet jogged over. "Let me show you how I hold it," she said.

Megan handed her the umbrella. But when Juliet tried to spin the umbrella, she winced. "Ow!" she said. "I can't do it. It hurts my wrist too much!"

"Don't worry, I'll try again," Megan said determinedly.

"You'll get there in the end," Sparkle said. "It just takes practice!"

Off they went again, around the ring. Megan tried holding the umbrella close. That made her lose her balance. But if she held it farther away, she couldn't twirl it at all!

"I'll try it in the other hand," she shouted to Juliet.

But this made her wobble even more. Sparkle swerved, but it was too late. With a thump, Megan landed in the sawdust.

Sparkle stopped at once and nuzzled her gently as Juliet ran over.

"Are you all right?" Juliet sounded very worried.

Megan felt like crying. She blinked her tears away and nodded. "I'm fine," she said, standing up and brushing sawdust off her leotard. "But I'll never be ready for the gala performance. I just can't do it!"

Chapter 5

Juliet looked like she might be ready to cry, too. "Well . . ." she said, in a small voice, "never mind. The clowns will have to do the grand finale instead."

Megan hung her head. She knew how much this meant to Juliet. She was sure that this was the task she was meant to do, but she had failed. She stroked Sparkle's mane. "I'm sorry I've let you down," she whispered. "The carousel must have chosen the wrong person."

Sparkle blew on her hair. "No, it didn't," he said, but for once he didn't sound quite so cheerful. "It must have taken Juliet a long time to learn her tricks. You've been trying to pick them up in just one day."

"How's it going?" called a voice from behind the curtain.

It was Joshua. He came into the ring and saw the look on their faces. "Oh dear," he said.

"I just can't get the hang of Juliet's tricks," Megan explained.

Joshua sighed. "It's been a bad day for everyone," he said. "I just heard that Clumpy the Clown has caught a cold."

"Oh no!" exclaimed Juliet. "Poor Clumpy. That means the clowns can't do the grand finale either!"

"I know," said Joshua. "But there's not much we can do about it now. It's getting late. Aunt Ellie sent me to tell you supper will soon be ready."

He looked at Megan curiously, and she blushed. She didn't have any supper to go to, and it was getting dark. Where was she supposed to go? But Sparkle leaned against her shoulder as though he could tell what she was thinking, and she knew he'd look after her somehow.

Juliet looked at Megan. "Why don't I ask Aunt Ellie if you can have supper with us?" she said.

"Oh, that's okay, I'm not hungry," said Megan hastily. She still felt a bit nervous about people asking her questions. In any case, she wanted to be alone so that she could talk to Sparkle properly.

"You have to eat *something*," said Juliet. "I just need to talk to her, that's all. If you don't mind waiting here, I'll be back as soon as I can."

Juliet and Joshua left the big top, and Megan turned to Sparkle. "What are we going to do?" she said. "Do we have to go back to the carousel?"

Sparkle blinked his big brown eyes. "Oh no, we can't go back yet!" he said, sounding shocked. "We have to complete the task first. We'll just have to keep practicing."

"I haven't even learned the first trick yet," said Megan. "I'll never learn them all in time."

The circus pony kneeled down in the sawdust. "Give it one more try," he said. "I'll do my best to canter really steadily."

Megan stroked Sparkle's neck. "I know you will," she said. "But I still don't think I can do it."

"Don't give up, Megan," Sparkle said.

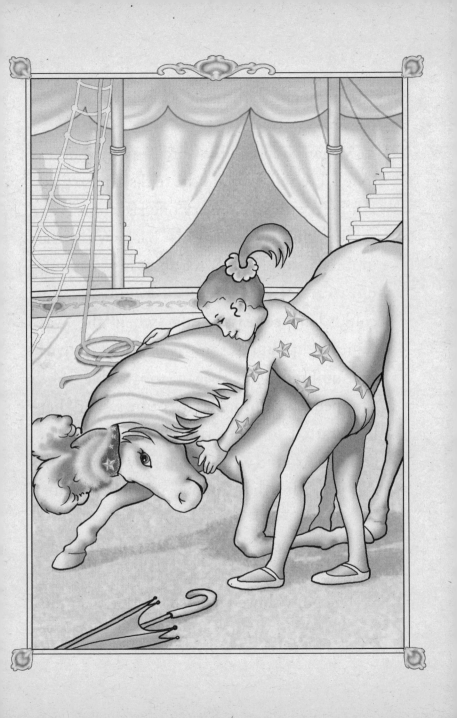

"Remember, the magic chose you for a reason."

Megan hugged the circus pony's neck. "Well, even if I *can't* do the tricks, I'm so glad I'm here with you. I'll try one last time."

She climbed onto his back with the umbrella, and Sparkle set off at his steadiest, most careful canter. Megan found that she could balance easily now when she was standing up, but as soon as she tried to twirl the umbrella, she began to wobble. She dropped the umbrella five times, and her legs started to ache with all the getting on and off. Around and around they went, until she was sure that Sparkle must be getting tired.

"It's no use, Sparkle," she sighed. "Let's stop now."

The pony slowed to a halt, and Megan slid

off his back. "We'll just have to go back," she said gloomily. She sat down in the sawdust. "You might still have time to find someone else before the grand finale."

Sparkle shook his head. "I'm not giving up," he said determinedly. "Let's try practicing a different trick."

"But Juliet's not here to teach me," Megan pointed out.

"Maybe Juliet's tricks aren't right for you," said Sparkle. "Is there anything else you could do?"

Megan thought hard. Suddenly she had an idea. "Maybe I could do something I know already, like my gymnastic moves!" she said, jumping up.

Sparkle pricked his ears. "Of *course*!" he exclaimed. "What can you do?"

"I'm quite good at handstands," she said.

"And I like working on the bar. I can do pivots and arabesques." Sparkle tipped his head to one side as if he didn't understand, so Megan explained, "Pivots are when you twirl around on the spot, and an arabesque is standing with one leg raised straight out behind you."

Her fingers and toes started to tingle. Maybe there was something she could do for the grand finale after all! But doing gymnastics on Sparkle's back was going to be very different from performing on a floor covered in rubber mats.

"I don't think I could do handstands," she warned Sparkle, "but I could try some arabesques. Look, I'll show you." First she did some stretches to warm up. Then she held on to her heel and lifted her foot so that her leg stuck straight up beside her head. "This is called a 'Y' balance," she puffed, "because I'm making the shape of a 'Y.' See?" She lowered her leg and tucked her arms by her sides to spin on a spot. "That's a pivot turn. I'm sure I could do that on your back. And I could som-ersault off at the end!"

Sparkle pranced on the spot, and Megan felt bubbles of excitement fizzing inside her. "I'll start with some cartwheels around the ring," she said. "If you were kneeling down, I could even vault onto your back!"

Sparkle tossed his head, making his head-dress shimmer in the lights. "Let's try!" he said, pawing the ground with his hoof.

Megan put the umbrella back behind the curtain, then cartwheeled back into the ring. Sparkle stood in the middle of the ring and trotted on the spot, lifting his hooves high in elegant little steps. Megan thought he looked beautiful! He kneeled down as

Megan cartwheeled toward him. She stood up and measured the distance in her mind, and with a one, two, three, she ran up to his back and vaulted right over.

"Brilliant!" Sparkle neighed.

In no time at all, the routine began to take shape. Once she was on his back, Megan soon got the hang of doing her gymnastics routines—an elegant arabesque, followed by a pivot turn, then bending down to touch her toes before stretching up with one leg to make a "Y." It was a lot easier than twirling the umbrella!

She was somersaulting off Sparkle's back when she heard a shout.

"Hey! What are you doing?" It was Juliet.

Megan looked down at the sawdust, feeling very awkward. Maybe she wasn't supposed to change Juliet's routine. "Sorry," she

said. "We were just trying something different. I hope you don't mind."

"*Mind?*" Juliet asked. She walked across
the ring, grinning from ear to ear. "Of course
I don't mind! This is going to be the best
performance *ever*!"

Chapter 6

Juliet gave Megan a hug. "Thank you, thank you!" she cried. "That routine is perfect for the grand finale. And guess what—I've talked to Aunt Ellie, and she says you can come for supper *and* stay the night."

"Oh! Are you sure she doesn't mind?" asked Megan, grinning in delight. She suddenly noticed how hungry she was.

"Quite sure," said Juliet. "Come on. Sparkle can spend the night with the other horses. He looks so much like Whisper that no one will notice."

After walking Sparkle to where all the other ponies were tied up, Megan followed Juliet to her brightly painted trailer, where Joshua and Aunt Ellie were waiting for them with a big homemade pizza steaming in the middle of the table.

"Lovely to meet you, Megan!" said Aunt Ellie. She was tall with smiling blue eyes. "I hear you're going to take Juliet's place—if the other riders are happy with your routine, of course."

Megan felt alarmed, and looked quickly at Juliet. She hadn't given a thought to the other riders!

"Don't worry," Juliet whispered. "We'll sort it out tomorrow. They'll all love your routine, I'm sure."

They tucked into the pizza, which was really tasty with lots of toppings and masses of cheese. When they'd finished, Megan felt much too sleepy to worry about the other riders. Juliet showed her the spare bunk, which had a pretty multicolored blanket and was right above where Juliet slept.

"It's the coziest bed I've ever seen!" exclaimed Megan.

Juliet smiled happily. "You can borrow some pajamas too," she said, pulling out a drawer from under her bunk. She handed Megan a pair of red-and-green-striped pajamas, and quickly the girls got changed.

Megan clambered up into the top bunk and wriggled under the beautiful blanket. The pillow was soft and comfortable. She was tired but very happy. Megan snuggled down and closed her eyes. . . .

* * *

When she opened them again it was morning. She pulled the curtain back and peered out of the tiny window next to her bunk. It was a beautiful sunny day with little fluffy clouds dotting the blue sky.

"Get up, get up!" cried Juliet, gently shaking Megan's leg through the blanket. "We've got lots to do before the performance!"

Megan jumped out of bed and put on the leotard and leggings that she had worn the day before. She helped Juliet to fetch Sparkle's morning feed before they went back into the trailer for breakfast. Aunt Ellie had been busy toasting some delicious homemade bread, and it smelled wonderful as they walked in.

"We'll get your costume first," said Juliet, as she buttered her toast. "Then you'll have plenty of time to rehearse in front of the other riders!"

Megan nodded eagerly, but she felt butterflies in her tummy at the thought of what they might say. Would they really think her act was good enough?

She finished her toast and drank her freshly squeezed orange juice, then followed Juliet outside again. The costume tent was close to the pony stables, and the sides of the tent had been rolled up, leaving just a stripy roof over the racks of clothes. Megan was pleased because it meant Sparkle could watch her try on the costume. She gave him a little wave as they skipped over the grass, and he whinnied happily.

Rows and rows of costumes in all colors of the rainbow filled the tent.

"Oh!" Megan gasped. "They're *gorgeous*!"

Juliet unhooked a hanger from near the end of a row. "This is my costume," she said.

Megan stared at it. The shiny pink leotard was decorated with tiny pearls and sequins, and a shimmering silvery skirt hung down from the waist in delicate, feathery wisps.

"Don't you like it?" Juliet said anxiously.

"Like it?" Megan managed to whisper. "Oh, Juliet, I *love* it."

"You'd better try it on," said Iris the costume lady. Megan recognized her at once—she was one of the Jolly Jugglers! "You can change behind this curtain," she said.

Megan's fingers shook as she pulled on the stunning costume. She was almost too scared to breathe in case it didn't fit. But it fitted perfectly—as if it had been made just for her. When she came out shyly, Juliet and Joshua were waiting to see how she looked.

"It's just right!" Juliet declared.

Joshua's eyes opened very wide. "Wow,

Megan!" he said. "You look great!"

Juliet showed Megan a mirror, and she gazed at herself in delight. She gave a little twirl, making the skirt float around her hips.

"Would you like me to add anything to the costume?" Iris asked with a friendly smile. "After all, you need to feel just right."

"Do you think we could have some feathery bits on the shoulders?" Megan said. "They'd look really pretty."

"Good idea," said Iris. "It will only take me a minute!"

Megan was so happy, she couldn't stop smiling. Carefully, she took the costume off and gave it to Iris, and slipped back into her leggings and leotard.

"I've got some feathers in my trailer," said Iris. "Juliet, could you come with me? I'll be quicker if I have someone to help."

Juliet nodded. "I won't be long," she said to Megan. "Do you want to stay here with Joshua? You could look at the other costumes."

"Yes, please!" said Megan, staring at the rows of colorful clothes.

Once Juliet and Iris had gone, Joshua flopped down on a trunk. "I'd better go and find the other acrobats soon," he said with a sigh. "I still haven't got the hang of the human pyramid."

"You've got all day to practice," Megan said.

Joshua shrugged. "I suppose so. I'll keep trying, but something tells me I'll never get it right."

Megan felt very sorry for him, because she'd felt exactly the same about twirling the umbrella. She was wondering what she could do to cheer him up when she heard a snort. She looked up.

Sparkle was poking his nose around the corner of the tent. "Look in the trunk!" he whispered.

"What—the one Joshua's sitting on?" Megan whispered back.

Sparkle nodded. Megan looked around to check that Joshua hadn't heard her talking to the circus pony. He hadn't. He looked as fed up as ever.

Megan noticed a bright red sleeve hanging out of the trunk. "What's that?" she asked, pointing.

"Another costume, I guess," said Joshua. He stood up and lifted the lid. The red sleeve belonged to a shiny, baggy clown outfit. The trousers were white with red dots, and the jacket was red with white dots and scarlet sleeves.

"Look at this!" Megan pulled out a wooden box full of colorful face paints. "It's clown makeup! Can I paint your face, Joshua? I did the makeup for our gymnastics display last term and everyone said I was really good."

"Okay," Joshua said. He held up the clown outfit and grinned. "I suppose you want me to dress up, too!"

Megan laughed. "Why not?"

Joshua started to pull the baggy spotted trousers over his leggings. His foot got caught, and he hopped about, trying to free it.

"I'm stuck!" he yelled. He looked so funny jumping around with his hair sticking up that Megan started to giggle.

"Let me help," she said between giggles.

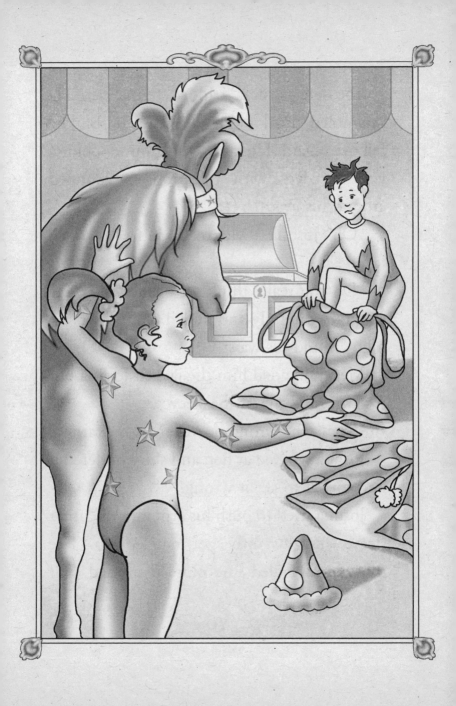

Too late: Joshua tripped right over! He scrambled up, looking determined. But he fell over again. He sat on the ground looking very puzzled, with the trousers wrapped around his legs.

"Oh, Joshua," Megan gasped. "You're so funny!"

"Do you really think so?" said Joshua. He stood up carefully and pulled the trousers up high around his waist.

Megan handed him the jacket. Joshua put his arm into one of the sleeves.

"That's the wrong sleeve!" Megan warned.

Joshua winked at her, and she wondered if he'd meant to get it wrong.

Joshua tried to push his arm into the other sleeve and instantly got tangled up. The more he wriggled, the more it seemed as if the jacket had come to life. It looked like he was struggling with a slippery red-and-white monster!

Megan thought she'd never seen anything so funny! She was laughing so hard that she didn't hear the footsteps walking across the grass toward her.

"What's going on here?" boomed a voice.

Megan jumped and looked up. Mr. Scarletti was standing at the edge of the tent, frowning.

Joshua went red. "S-sorry, Mr. Scarletti," he stuttered. He tried to untangle himself, but all the wriggling only made his trousers fall down. Luckily he still had his leggings on underneath.

"It's my fault," Megan said quickly. "Playing with the costumes was my idea."

To her surprise, a smile spread over Mr. Scarletti's face. "Well, well, well," he said. "I think we've just found another clown!"

Megan thought about the way Joshua had tumbled around the tent, making his costume come to life. Of course! He'd make a *much* better clown than an acrobat!

"Why don't you speak to the other clowns?" suggested Mr. Scarletti. "Clumpy is too ill to perform, so I'm sure they'll be glad to fit you into their routine."

Joshua beamed. "Really, Mr. Scarletti? Thank you!"

Mr. Scarletti walked away, twirling his long black cane, and Joshua ran off to find the other clowns. Just before he disappeared behind a trailer, Megan saw him turn a cartwheel from excitement.

She wrapped her arms around Sparkle's

neck. "You knew this would happen when you told me to look in the trunk, didn't you?" she whispered. "You really are the cleverest pony in the world!"

Chapter 7

Sparkle snuffled warmly in her hair. "You gave me the idea when you decided to use gymnastics in our routine," he said. "I knew Joshua would be good at something—it just wasn't being an acrobat."

"Let's go and tell Juliet," Megan said.

As they headed toward the trailers, one of the doors opened and Juliet bounded out.

"Megan! We've finished!" she called. "The costume's going to be *wonderful*!"

"We've got some news for you, too,"

Megan said. "Joshua and I were playing with the clown costumes. He was so funny, Mr. Scarletti said he could take Clumpy's place in the show tonight!"

"With the clowns?" Juliet said. "That's a brilliant idea!" She gave Megan a hug. "Iris was just telling me that the acrobats were going to give up on the human pyramid, because it wasn't working. They're going to do their usual routine instead."

Megan clapped her hands together. "Then everything's working out perfectly!" She laughed.

But then she felt those butterflies in her tummy again. There was still one more thing. She had to convince the other riders that she was good enough to take Juliet's place.

* * *

The rehearsal took place in the big top. Sparkle trotted along with five of the other ponies, and Juliet introduced Megan to their riders—Sally, Jameela, Andy, Clara, and Raj. They were friendly, but Megan could see that she would have to do her very best if she was going to impress them.

"Come on, then, let's see what you're made of!" said Jameela.

Juliet smiled encouragingly, and Megan began her routine. It went even better than it had the night before. As she did her final somersault, Megan heard everyone clapping, and she breathed a sigh of relief.

"Well done!" called Raj. "We'll be proud to have you with us!"

"Did you hear that, Sparkle?" whispered Megan. "I think it means that we're on!"

* * *

Once the other riders had gone through their tricks, Megan and Juliet took Sparkle to the stables to get him ready. Juliet couldn't get her sling wet so Megan washed his mane and tail, then brushed them until they felt like silk. Juliet carefully oiled his hooves, and last of all they put on his twinkling pink head-dress.

"You look beautiful!" Megan declared.

Sparkle whinnied and tossed his head.

Juliet turned to Megan. "Come on, it's your turn now!"

They went to Iris's trailer, where Megan put on her beautiful costume. Iris brushed glitter onto her cheeks and silvery blue eye shadow onto her eyelids, then finished off with some pretty pink lipstick.

"Is that really me?" Megan breathed, staring into the mirror.

"Yes, it's really you," said Juliet. "You look like a princess!"

Megan took a deep breath. It was half past five—nearly time for the show to start. "Should I go to the big top now?" she asked.

Juliet nodded and took Megan's hand. "Don't worry, I'll come with you. We can peep through the curtains and watch people arrive."

They fetched Sparkle from the stables and walked over to the big top. The rows of seats were quickly filling up with people. Soon only the seat for the guest of honor was empty. Mr. Scarletti appeared with a man wearing a red cloak and a big gold chain.

"That's the mayor!" Juliet whispered.

Megan gulped. She didn't want to make any mistakes in front of such an important person.

Mr. Scarletti waited until the mayor was sitting down in the empty seat, then came behind the curtain. "Hurry up, everyone!" he called. "Only ten minutes to go!" He gave Megan a wink.

The show was about to start!

Mr. Scarletti strode into the ring. "Ladies and gentlemen, you have come to the most incredible, the most fantastic, the most extraordinary show on earth!" he boomed. "Mr. Scarletti's Amazing Traveling Circus will astonish you and fill you with wonder . . . so without further ado, please welcome our first performance—the mind-boggling, bemusing, and bewitching Ivor the Illusionist!"

A man in a big black cloak ran past Megan into the ring, and she recognized the person in the leopard-skin leotard that she'd seen yesterday. He looked pretty different now!

She and Juliet hid behind the curtain while the first few performers went on. They heard the crowd gasp as Carrie the Contortionist tied herself in knots. She backflipped out, beaming.

"Great audience!" she puffed as she flipped past Megan and Juliet.

The Jolly Jugglers went in next. Megan peeped through the curtain and saw them throwing burning fire sticks to each other, so the air was full of flickering flames. She'd never seen anything like it.

After the jugglers, it was the clowns' turn. Megan hardly recognized Joshua. His face was white with big black eyebrows and a huge red smile. But she knew it was him because he was smaller than all the others, and she could still see black tufts of hair peeping out from under his pointy red and yellow hat.

"Good luck, Joshua!" she called. "You can do it." She peeped through the curtains to watch him.

He was brilliant! The crowd howled with laughter as Joshua squirted himself in the eye with a trick flower, fell off a ladder when he was trying to hang up a flag, and tumbled out of the clowns' collapsing car. When he came running out through the curtain, his painted smile looked wider than ever!

There were only three more acts before Megan's turn. A team of trapeze artists swung from one to another high up near the roof of the tent. Then Sticky the Stilt-walker, who still looked grumpy, stalked around and rode a unicycle, still wearing his stilts. He was followed by the acrobats, who gave a well-practiced performance without Joshua.

At last Mr. Scarletti strode into the ring, and the crowd went quiet. The butterflies in Megan's tummy started fluttering like mad.

Mr. Scarletti beamed at his audience. "Ladies and gentlemen, it's the grand finale! Please give a warm welcome to our Prancing Ponies."

Juliet gave Megan a hug with her good arm. "Good luck. You'll be fine," she whispered.

Megan smiled. "I know Sparkle will look after me," she whispered back.

The drums began to roll, and the other ponies cantered into the ring. Sparkle trotted in last of all, the only one without a rider. Megan heard the crowd murmur in surprise. *It's just a gymnastics performance,* she told herself. *You've done this lots of time before!*

Taking a deep breath, she smoothed down her glittery skirt and checked the feathers on her shoulders. Then she followed Sparkle through the red curtain. This was it! She was the star performer at Mr. Scarletti's Amazing Traveling Circus!

At first, the lights were so bright she couldn't see the audience at all. She stood in the ring, blinking. The whole big top was quiet, waiting for the grand finale to begin.

There was another drum roll, and Megan began to cartwheel around the ring just inside the circle of cantering ponies. Sparkle waited in the middle, trotting prettily on the spot. His neck was arched, and his shimmering headdress seemed to flash with little stars under the big lights. Megan's heart swelled with pride, and suddenly she wasn't nervous anymore. When she had cartwheeled one complete circle, he kneeled down and she vaulted right over his back. The applause rippled around the tent as the crowd clapped and cheered. They loved it!

With a one, two, three, Megan vaulted onto Sparkle's back, and he stood up with a toss of his headdress.

As they cantered around with the other ponies, Megan spotted Juliet peeping through the curtain. She grinned and gave Megan a thumbs-up. Then Megan had to concentrate hard again. The atmosphere in the big top was electric, and all eyes were on Megan as she rode around. Sparkle's ears were pricked, and she knew he was ready for her to stand up. He gave an encouraging snort as she got to her feet and carefully stretched one leg behind her in a perfect arabesque.

Putting her foot down, she kept her legs dead straight while she touched her toes. She twirled to the back, and back to the front.

The music rose and fell, and the crowd began to clap in time. Around and around Sparkle cantered, without making a single mistake. It was the most wonderful night of Megan's life!

"Well done," she heard Sparkle say, as she stretched her leg up to make a "Y" shape.

"I could never have done it without you," Megan said to him, as she brought her leg down again.

The grand finale was almost over. The music built up to a crescendo as the ponies cantered around one last time. Then, through the curtain, she saw Mr. Scarletti standing next to Juliet. He lifted his top hat to her and grinned. Megan was so glad she hadn't let his circus down!

She breathed in the sharp smell of sawdust and waved with both hands, gazing in delight at the sea of happy smiles. It was over—Sparkle was heading for the beautiful red velvet curtain, and Megan gave one final wave. But as they cantered out of the ring, Sparkle's thundering hoofbeats suddenly faded. Instead of the roaring crowd, Megan heard the faint sound of fairground music. The air filled with glittering pink and silver sparkles that slowly cleared away.

Megan looked around. There was no sign of Juliet or Mr. Scarletti. She was back on the Magic Carousel, riding Sparkle the carousel pony. Her beautiful costume had vanished, and she was wearing her jeans and jacket again. And there was her mom, smiling and waving as the carousel slowed down.

When the carousel finally came to a halt, Megan slipped off Sparkle and patted his neck. It felt like sleek painted wood now. Something tickled Megan's neck. She reached under her collar and pulled out a soft, pink feather that must have fallen off her costume. "It's mine to keep!" Megan gasped. Now she would have a bit of the circus with her forever.

"Thank you, Sparkle," she whispered. "That was the most amazing adventure I've ever had in my life. I'll never, never forget it!"

And just for a moment, she was sure his ears twitched in reply.

Chapter 1

S uddenly, there it was.

In a corner of the field, tucked behind a pink-and-white-striped cotton candy stand, stood an old-fashioned pony carousel. It was painted a rich red, with touches of gold and silver, and a scarlet flag fluttered from the pointy golden roof. Gorgeous wooden ponies cantered around and around, rising and falling on twisty golden poles in time to the music. As soon as Amy saw it, she knew *this* was the perfect first ride.

Amy ran over to look more closely at the different ponies. There were so many! Each pony's name was painted onto a little scroll that hung from the twisty pole rising from its back. There was a white circus pony called Sparkle, who had feathers nodding on his headdress and a mischievous glint in his eye. Next to Sparkle was a chestnut pony named Star, with a lasso hanging from her saddle— she must be a cowgirl's pony!

But there, just behind Star, was the pony Amy wanted to ride most of all. He was a magnificent dark bay pony with a proudly arched neck and flaring nostrils. He looked noble and adventurous, and his big brown eyes seemed to look straight at Amy, inviting her to climb aboard. His name scroll said *Brightheart*, and it was the perfect name for him.